ER
Wo
Woodman

Whose birthday is it?

Whose Birthday Is It?

Whose Birthday Is It?

by
Bill Woodman

Thomas Y. Crowell

New York

Library of Congress Cataloging in Publication Data

Woodman, Bill.
Whose birthday is it?
SUMMARY: Bob Bear is invited to a birthday party,
but he doesn't know whose birthday it is or where the
party will be.
[1. Birthdays—Fiction.   2. Animals—Fiction]
I. Title.
PZ7.W8604Wh   [E]   79-2776
ISBN 0-690-04005-9   ISBN 0-690-04006-7 lib. bdg.

10 9 8 7 6 5 4 3 2 1
First Edition

To Barbara,
Jowill, and Anne

Early one morning

Elmer Fox delivered the mail.

Knock, knock!

"Mail call, mail call,"

said Elmer.

"What's this? A letter for me?"

said Bob Bear.

"Oh, my goodness,

I've been invited

to a birthday party.

But whose birthday is it?"

"I'll need a gift.

I'll take honey.

Honey always makes a nice gift."

Bob Bear stepped out into the snow.

"Brr-rr, it's cold," he said.

"Who would have a birthday

in the middle of winter?"

"Hey, Donald! Donald Rabbit!

Whose birthday is it?"

But before Bob could get an answer,

Don was gone.

On Bob went through
the snowy woods.
Soon he met the Raccoon Twins.
"Hi, Jeff," said Bob.

"Hi, Jerry.

Which way to the party?"

"This way," said Jerry.

"That way," said Jeff.

Bob didn't know which way to go.

"I'd better sit down and rest a minute," he thought.

"Gee, it sure is pretty here by the pond."

"HI, BOB! WHATCHA DOING?"

It was George the Moose.

"SAY, BOB, YOU GOING
TO THE PARTY?"

23

"YIPE!" said Bob.

And through the ice he went.

"Going to the party?

Follow me," said a beaver.

"It's up this hill."

Bob ran after the beaver.

"For two cents I'd go home!"

he said.

Then Bob saw a cabin.

"Why, that's my cabin!" he said.

"Home at last!"

He started to run.

33

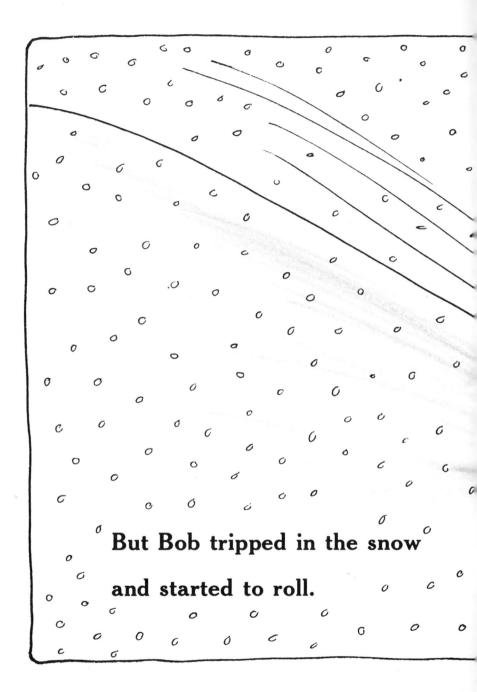

But Bob tripped in the snow
and started to roll.

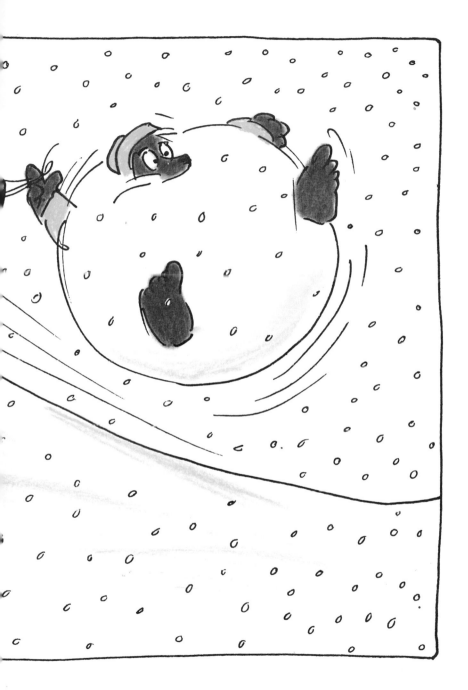

Meanwhile, at the cabin,

a party was getting under way.

There was a thump at the door.

"I'll get it," said the beaver.

And in came Bob.

41

It was the best birthday

Bob ever had.